Findus Moves Out

Sven Nordqvist

HAWTHORN PRESS

The morning sun shone on Pettson's little farm. The birds chirruped and sang. Bumblebees were already awake and buzzing among the apple blossoms, and from the hen house came a faint clucking.
But there was another noise. One you don't normally hear in the countryside.
It went thump-squeak-thump-squeak-thump-squeak. It came from Pettson's house.

Ordinary people sleep at four o'clock in the morning. But in Pettson's bedroom there was someone quite out of the ordinary, and that was Findus the cat. Findus had got a bed of his own, you see. A real little bed with a nice springiness to it, which he really liked to bounce on. As soon as he woke up, he began to bounce. Thump-squeak-thump-squeak-thump-squeak.
Pettson twisted and turned and tried to hide under his pillow.
`What a horrible racket!' He sputtered and sat up. `FINDUS! If you must make that noise, then do it quietly! Remember what you promised yesterday!'

Findus stopped bouncing. He thought carefully.

`Not to sit on the chimney?' he said.

`No, that's not what I meant, said Pettson. I mean the same thing you promised the day before yesterday and the day before that.'

`Not to … tease the chickens?'

`No!'

`Not … to …' As he thought he bounced a bit. Carefully.

`You promised to stop jumping on the bed at four o'clock in the morning!'

`Is it only four o'clock? I thought it was only half past.'

`It makes no difference,' said Pettson. `It's too early for bouncing on beds. You woke me up just like you've done every morning since you got that bed. Either you stop jumping or … we move the bed out somewhere else.'

`Either stop jumping … or move?' said Findus.

`Either or,' said Pettson.

Findus thought for a moment. Then he said:

`Then I'll move.'

Pettson stared at him.

'Move?' he said. 'You can't move out just like that, can you?'

'Course I can. If I'm not allowed to jump on the bed I can,' said Findus.

'But … you could jump after I wake up?'

'Impossible! A cat needs to do his morning exercise as soon as he wakes up. Otherwise he gets all stiff like an old man and hobbles around complaining.'

'Yes, but still …' said Pettson, '… move out? How can you think of such a thing? Where will you live?'

'Well, I don't know … in a house maybe,' said Findus. 'Don't you have an old house lying around somewhere, Pettson? A little house, quite big. Like a tall cabin, but smaller. It should be … THIS big,' he said, jumping as high as he could.

`That sounds just like the old outhouse on the hill,' said Pettson.
`But that's an old loo!' said Findus, stopping in mid-jump. `I can't live
in a loo. What if I'm jumping on my bed and bounce down the hole.
Right down into the poop bucket! And besides, it's too far away.'
`We'll take care of that. I can move it here to the garden and tidy it up.'
Pettson had perked up at the thought of having something to fix.
`Hmm, we'll see,' said Findus.
`If you cover the hole, maybe …'

After breakfast, Pettson fetched the outhouse. It wasn't very heavy, so he just tipped it onto a wheelbarrow and trundled it down to the garden. He pulled up planks and sawed and hammered, and by afternoon the house was finished.

It was time to carry in the bed.
Findus tested the bounce height. The house was the right size for
jumping in. He didn't hit the ceiling, and the hole and bucket were gone.
'It's a fine house, Pettson,' he said. 'You're nice.'
'Yes, well,' Pettson muttered. 'I do like to sleep a bit longer than you in
the mornings.'

Findus spent the whole day in his little house. He jumped and tidied a bit and jumped again, and chased out a spider, and jumped some more. Then the hens came wanting to jump as well, but they weren't allowed.

He so enjoyed being in his new house that he completely forgot about Pettson.
Later in the evening the old man came and knocked on the door.
`Come in and have some supper,' he said.
Findus was in very high spirits and bunny-hopped all the way to the big house.
`I need a small table and a chair,' he said, `So I can eat supper in my own house.
But today I can sit and eat on the bed.'
`But … you're not even going to eat at home?' Pettson said.`Isn't it enough to ju–?'
But Findus was already in the kitchen getting his porridge. Then he took it back
out to his house. Disappointed, Pettson watched him go.

The old man sat alone in the kitchen with his porridge.

`It is awfully quiet without a cat,' he thought.`How strange. To think of all those poor souls sitting alone without a cat. Poor me. Let's see if I can hear him.'

He opened the kitchen door. After a while he could hear the faint thuds of Findus jumping.

`Yes, he's out there, all right,' Pettson thought. `He'll come in if he gets lonely.'

He ate some spoonfuls of porridge. It was as quiet as it had been before Findus ever came to live with him.

`But what if I get lonely?' Pettson wondered. `I can hardly go and sleep out there. But I will go and say goodnight.'

He went out and knocked on the door and peeked inside. Findus had stopped jumping. He was straightening the bed for the night.

`Are you alright, Findus?' Pettson said.

`Yes, but this bed's a mess,' the cat said. `Are you going to sleep now?'

`Yes, I just wanted to say goodnight.'

`Goodnight.'

`See you tomorrow,' Pettson said.

`Sure. Close the door now,' Findus said. He wasn't being rude, just a bit distracted. He had other things to think about.

Pettson sighed. He went inside and lay down in his quiet bedroom.

`Things are as they are. At least I get to sleep in a little tomorrow morning. Sweet dreams, old man.'

Pettson dreamt of a little green-striped cat that bounced soundlessly on a soft lawn. High, soaring leaps right up to the clouds.

He woke when Findus came in and started jumping on his bed.

`Wake up, old man! It's fifty o'clock! Time for breakfast!' the cat whooped.

`Alright, alright, take it easy,' Pettson said. 'Did you sleep well in your new house?'

`I did, but it needs some wallpaper. You must help me spruce it up, because I'm having guests today.'

`Really? Who?' Pettson said.

`Wait and see. It's a secret,' Findus said. `I'm having a house-warming party and you're going to help me make pancakes. Later. First we need to put up some wallpaper.'

After breakfast they went up to the attic and dug out some old rolls of wallpaper. Then they both helped put it up. The hens wanted to help as well, but they weren't allowed. They were not very good at wallpapering. Instead they ate some wallpaper paste, which they enjoyed.

Afterwards, Pettson put in a stool, to serve as a table, and a little stool, to serve as a little stool.

Findus was very pleased with his new house.

During the day he was there a lot, jumping on his bed or putting up a picture or fixing something. But now and then he came out and helped Pettson weed the vegetable patch.

`I'm hungry,' Findus said, `which means my guest must be coming soon. You'd better make pancakes now.'

`Won't you say who's coming? I'm really curious,' Pettson said.

`It's forbidden to tell secrets, I'm afraid. But you'll find out soon. I'll tell you when the pancakes are done.'

Pettson lit the stove and began to mix the batter.

`Is another cat coming?' he tried.

`Nooo,' Findus said.

`The hens?' Pettson said.

`The hens!? Oh no! They'd just babble and gobble everything up!'

Pettson carried on guessing while he fried the pancakes, but he couldn't figure out who the guest was.

`Are they ready?' Findus said. `Now I'll tell you. It's you! You're the one who's invited to dinner at my house. Right now!'

`Thank you, thank you very much! I would never have thought that I'd be invited to a pancake party!' Pettson said, giving a bow.

`It wasn't that hard to figure out,' Findus said.

They walked over to the little house, taking the pancakes and jam and two glasses of milk. Then they sat and ate, and Findus thought he had arranged it all very well. (In fact, the old man had helped a bit as well.)

`It's good we live so close, so you can come and visit now and then,' Pettson said. `It felt a little empty last night with you not at home.'

`But I still live at home. I've only moved,' Findus said.

`Really...? That's good,' Pettson said. `So it's not so very different from before?'

`Nope. It's just like before,' Findus said. `Only I've moved. To another house, that is. But I still live at home.'

`Well … I see … ' Pettson hesitated. `So the only difference is that I can't hear you bouncing on the bed?'

`Exactly!' Findus said.

`Well, THAT's good. So I suppose I have to put up with a bit of quiet in the evenings too.'

They sat silent for a moment, looking at the wallpaper.

`Thanks for a delicious dinner,' Pettson said. `It's been ages since I was treated to such tasty pancakes. Now I must go and shut the hens in. Are you coming?'

`Of course I'm coming,' Findus said.

They made the evening rounds and put away all the shovels and old wallpaper rolls and shut the hens in. Then they went into the kitchen and Pettson listened to the weather forecast on the radio. After that, Pettson read an old story called Puss-in-Boots. Findus sat on his lap and listened. The fire in the woodstove crackled and smelt nice. It was lovely and quiet. When he'd finished the story, Pettson said:

`Well, Findus, it's my bedtime. And you're heading out to sleep in your own house, I suppose?'

`Yeees … I suppose …' the cat said.

He didn't sound particularly pleased.

Findus dragged his feet towards the door. He stopped there and looked at the old man.

`Come out with me!' he said.

`Are you scared of the dark?' Pettson said.

`No, but … I've got something to show you.'

Pettson went with Findus to the little house.

　　　`Look,' Findus said.

　　　　He did a jump. It was nothing special. He had done better ones before.

　　　　　He probably just wanted company a little while longer, Pettson thought.

　　　　　　`That was good,' he said. `Goodnight, cat. Sleep well.'

　　　　　　　`Goodnight, old man. See you tomorrow,' Findus said.

Findus lay listening to the silence and couldn't sleep. It was as if the silence was filled with a lot of silent rustlings, and he didn't know what he wasn't hearing. Eventually he ran in to Pettson, who had gone to bed.

`I thought I heard the fox!' said Findus.

`He can't get in if you lock the door,' said Pettson.

`But I can't sleep if there's a fox at the door,' Findus said.

`Of course not,' Pettson said. `We'll have to think of something, then. But it's late now. We'll do it tomorrow.'

`I want to sleep here tonight,' Findus said.

`You may. If you behave.'

`Oh yes. I always behave,' Findus said, nestling down at the foot of the bed.

`Can I sleep here? I won't jump, I promise. I'll just lie completely still.'

`That's fine,' Pettson said. `Good night.'

Next morning at four o'clock, Findus woke as bright as always. At once, he began bouncing on the bed. It just happened, even though he had promised to behave. Pettson woke, sour as a radish.

`Findus!' the old man growled.

`It wasn't me, I'm leaving now,' Findus said and darted out to his own house, where he could jump as much as he liked.

Eventually, Pettson woke himself up and wasn't cross anymore.

They were going to build an alarm to scare away all the foxes. They fastened tripwires around Findus's house, with bells that tinkled if you tripped on them. And they hung lanterns in the trees and Findus borrowed a rattle that made an awful din. This would wake Pettson and scare away the fox, if there was one.

Findus tested the tripwires and the rattle a few times, but otherwise he was hardly in his house all day. He only jumped on the bed once.

In the evening they made the usual rounds. Then they sat in the kitchen, listening to music on the radio. Findus lay on the sofa and was so comfortable that he fell asleep. He woke when Pettson turned off the radio to go to bed.

'So, Findus. It's late,' he said. 'You'd better go out and get some sleep, so you can get up at four in the morning and jump on the bed.'

Findus was quiet and sleepy and didn't look at all happy.

'There's probably loads and loads of foxes out tonight, there normally is on Wednesdays,' he said.

'Today is not Wednesday,' Pettson said. 'And we'll light the lanterns, and we fixed the tripwires and everything.'

'Yes, but … there are mice …' Findus said. 'Special mice that gnaw through tripwires. They live on tripwires, actually. Can't I sleep here again tonight, and we'll think of something better tomorrow?'

'Sure, if you can manage not to jump on the bed in the morning …' Pettson said.

'Oh yes, I promise,' Findus said. 'I'll go out when I wake up. Right away!'

'That's settled then,' Pettson said.

At four o'clock the next morning, Findus woke as usual and looked out the window. It was pouring with rain and not even properly light yet. `Rats! It looks wet,' he thought. `Should I really I go out there just to jump on a bed? I'd rather sleep some more.'

He went back to sleep and didn't see Pettson peeking slyly at him, smiling.

When they woke at seven o'clock, they didn't mention Findus's house
or jumping on beds. At breakfast Pettson said:

`Shall we bring in your bed again?'

`Yes, maybe we should,' Findus said.

`So you'll do your jumping during the day in future?' Pettson said.

`Yes, at five o'clock.'

`No, that's too early. When I've woken up.'

`Six o'clock?'

`No. Seven,' Pettson said. `Seven at the earliest.'

`Okay. Seven. When is seven o'clock?' Findus said.

`You don't know how to tell the time?' Pettson said. `What kind of a cat
can't tell the time? Well then, I'll teach you.'

And so Findus learnt to tell the time – but that is another story.

Illustrator Sven Nordqvist and his odd creations Pettson and Findus are household names in their native Sweden and beyond. Over the past two decades their books have been translated into 44 languages and read by millions (It can take a while for us English-speakers to catch up with what the rest of the world is reading). Cranky old Pettson and his stripey-trousered cat have developed a cult following among both children and adults, and when you meet them you'll understand why.

Books suitable for ages 3 to 99.

© Photo: Stefan Nilsson

Ordering books

If you have difficulties ordering Hawthorn Press books from a bookshop, you can order online at www.hawthornpress.com or direct from:

United Kingdom
Booksource
Tel: (0845) 370 0063 Fax: (0845) 370 0064 E-mail: orders@booksource.net

OTHER FINDUS AND PETTSON BOOKS FROM HAWTHORN PRESS

PANCAKES FOR FINDUS
Sven Nordqvist

It is Findus' birthday, so Farmer Pettson wants to bake a big stack of pancakes for him. But before he can start, Pettson has to fix a puncture in his bike, find the keys to the shed and distract Anderson's bull. Only then can he bike to the shop to buy flour for the pancakes.

28pp; 297 × 210mm; 978-1-903458-79-2; hb

WHEN FINDUS WAS LITTLE AND DISAPPEARED
Sven Nordqvist

Farmer Pettson lives with his hens in an old red farmhouse. He sometimes feels lonely. One day his neighbour Mrs Anderson visits with the present of a tiny kitten in a cardboard box labelled *Findus Green Peas* ...

28pp; 297 × 210mm; 978-1-903458-83-9; hb

FINDUS AND THE FOX
Sven Nordqvist

There's a hen-hunting fox on the loose. But farmer Pettson and his quirky cat Findus agree that foxes shouldn't be killed. They should be tricked. They come up with a fabulous plan, which makes for an explosive, unforgettable night.

28pp; 297 × 210mm; 978-1-903458-87-7; hb

FINDUS GOES CAMPING
Sven Nordqvist

One day, Findus finds a tent in the attic. Pettson starts imagining how it will be going camping by the lake, catching fish and grilling them over the fire as the sun sets. This is not exactly how things turn out, as Findus, Pettson and the hens try hiking – in the garden.

28pp; 297 × 210 mm; 978-1-903458-91-4: hb

FINDUS AT CHRISTMAS
Sven Nordqvist

It is the day before Christmas Eve and Pettson and his talking cat Findus have lots to do, but disaster strikes when Pettson sprains his ankle. How can they celebrate Christmas now – with no tree, ham, meatballs or gingerbread? For all their resourcefulness, Findus and Pettson are close to giving up, when suddenly there is a knock on the door ...

28pp; 297 × 210mm; 978-1-907359-05-7; hb